A Bed for Bug

📖 Just Right Reader

A big red bug is on his bed.

The red bug is big.
His bed is not.

"I have to have a big
bed," said the red bug.
"My leg will not fit."

The red bug sits up.

"My bed is not big."

The red bug is big!

The bed is NOT big.

He will get rid of his bed and get a big bed.

He will jet to get a bed.

The bug looks for a big bed.

The tan bed is BIG.

The tin bed is NOT big.

He will not get the tan bed.

He will not get the tin bed.

The red bed fits him.

His leg fits.

Bug is set on his big red bed.

Phonics Fun

- Write one of the words from the book (e.g., bed).
- Write the word again, but change the first letter (e.g., change the B to R).
- What is the new word (e.g., red)?

 Comprehension

How did the bug behave at the beginning of the story?

 High Frequency Words

have   will

of

 Decodable Words

bed	leg
get	red
jet	set